Published by Semiotext(e)
PO BOX 629, South Pasadena, CA 91031
www.semiotexte.com

Special thanks to Bruce Hainley

Cover: Richard Hawkins, *Stairwell Down* (detail), 2007. Altered dollhouse and table, 42 ¾ x 36 ¾ x 36 ¾ inches. Courtesy of the artist.

Design: Hedi El Kholti
ISBN: 978-1-63590-137-5

Distributed by the MIT Press, Cambridge, MA, and London, England.
Printed and bound in the United States of America.
10 9 8 7 6 5 4 3

Castle Faggot

Derek McCormack

Afterword by
Dennis Cooper and Zac Farley

semiotext(e)

For Jack

FAGGOTLAND

WELCOME

Welcome to Doodyland! Faggotland's your land! Funland's for fun, Futureland's for futures, Fantasticland's fantastic— Faggotland's for faggots!

FAGGOTLAND

Walt Doody designed Faggotland for faggots. It looks like Paris, the faggiest city. It looks like Monstermartre, the faggiest part of the city. It's the part for faggots and monsters—and faggot monsters!

FAGGOTS OF FAGGOTLAND

Vive le Faggotland! It's full of all your faggot favorites— Count Choc-o-log, Boo-Brownie, Franken-Fudge and a fuckload of their friends. They're the monster mascots of breakfast cereals you faggots buy!

COUNT CHOC-O-LOG

The king of Faggotland's Count Choc-o-log. Castle Faggot's his castle. It's a haunted castle—go through it and get the shit scared out of you. What's so scary? The castle's full of dead faggots. What did they die of? They ate Count Choc-o-log cereal!

SHIT

Shit, shit, shit! Shit's the flavor of Faggotland. There are shitty rides, shitty restaurants, shitty shops. There are restrooms— shitloads of shitty restrooms. There are turds in the toilets, turds in the sinks. There are seven turds in this sentence!

RIDES OF FAGGOTLAND

If you like rides with puerile puns for names, Faggotland's for you. There's Castle Faggot. Also: Count Choc-o-log's Log Ride, Boo-Brownie's Buttfuck Bumper Cars, Franken-Fudge's Faggot Fun Slide.

FOODS OF FAGGOTLAND

If you like fancy French cuisine, Faggotland's for you. Le Mâche-Merde, Faggotland's finest café, specializes in cuisine made from Count Choc-o-log cereal: crêpes that taste like crap; custard farts. Boo-Brownie's Brownery sells brownies; Franken-Fudge's Fudgery sells fudge.

SHOPS OF FAGGOTLAND

If you like fancy French crap, Faggotland's for you. At Charles Baudéclair's perfume shop, Les Fleurs du Mallomar, you can buy scents that smell like cocoa and shit; at Jean Profitelorrain's sex shop, you can buy shit-flavoured condoms and chocolate-coated toilet paper; at Stéphane Marshmallarmé's bookshop, you can buy shit like books.

YOUR PERSONAL GUIDE TO FAGGOTLAND

You can locate the landmarks by referring to this flyer.

·

1. Fag Gates   2. Place du Ass   3. Sacré Cul Cathedral
4. Arse de Triomphe   5. The Loo Museum   6. Toiletries
Garden   7. Sore Bum University   8. Palais de la Shitty
9. Sharts Cathedral   10. Le Mâche-Merde Café   11. Le
Mal Marché Monster Department Store   12. Statue of
Count Choc-o-log   13. Castle Faggot

CASTLE FAGGOT

Faggots!—kill yourselves!

Kill yourselves at Doodyland!

Kill yourselves at Faggotland, the faggiest land in Doodyland.

Funland's for fun, Futureland's for futures, Fantasticland's fantastic—Faggotland's for faggots.

Kill yourselves at Castle Faggot, the faggiest ride in Faggotland.

Castle Faggot—it's a haunted house with a faggoty theme. At a haunted house, there are ghosts; at Castle Faggot, there are faggots—faggots and also cartoons. The faggots are dead faggots who came to the castle to commit suicide; the cartoons are animatronic. They're fagimatronic!

Count Choc-o-log's the cartoon king of the castle. He's a vampire. He's the mascot of a breakfast cereal faggots buy. It's supposed to taste like chocolate; instead it tastes like shit. Faggots love chocolate; faggots love shit.

What else do faggots love? Suicide!

Castle Faggot's the faggiest place to commit suicide.

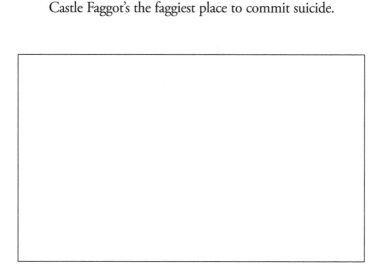

Castle Faggot's a fairy tale castle, but brown—bats burst from it like brown fireworks.

Bats! Rats! It's Count Choc-o-log's castle; it's crawling with his creatures. The bats are faggot bats; the rats are faggot rats. They feed on the flies and dead faggots that fill the place. It's a feast.

All these dead faggots! All these dead fucking faggots! They're crammed into every corner of the castle. There are dead faggots in the tower. They're caked in their own blood. There are dead faggots in the library. They're caked in their own shit. The ballroom? There's a faggot hanging from the chandelier.

That faggot's more chandelier than faggot!

Why do faggots commit suicide? Why not?

All the faggots in the castle died because they wanted to be décor.

A faggot hangs himself—he's décor; a faggot slits his wrists—he's décor; a faggot shoots himself in the head—he's décor.

What do you call a faggot hanging from a chandelier? Crystal.

What do you call a faggot with a hole in his head? Vase.

Why, there are so many ways for faggots to die, and so many dead faggots—at Faggotland, they end up doing what they dreamed of: decorating a castle at the Faggot Kingdom!

Kill yourselves at Castle Faggot!

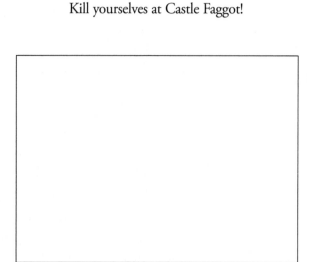

You'll see Count Choc-o-log—he's chocolate-brown; you'll see Boo-Brownie and Franken-Fudge, mascots of similar monster cereals—Boo's blueberry-blue, Frank's strawberry-pink!

You'll see Count Froufrou, an interior decorator to the undead—he decorated the castle for Count Choc-o-log!

He decorated it as a crypt.

"*Bienvenue!*"

Count Choc-o-log greets you in the foyer. He bows and says *bienvenue*. He bows and says *bienvenue*. He bows and says *bienvenue*.

There's a speaker in his ass.

Count Choc-o-log's in the gallery. It's hung with portraits of Count Choc-o-log. They're all painted by faggots who killed themselves. They're all painted with the same palette: shit brown, shit blue, shit pink.

The paintings are shit.

Count Choc-o-log's in the library. It's bursting with books about Count Choc-o-log. They're all written by faggots who killed themselves. They're all bound in faggot skin. There's a book with an eye. There's a book with an eyebrow. There's a book with an asshole: it farts and starts to shit. The writing's shit.

Delishit!

The chandelier! It's crystal. It's brown crystal. It's smeared with shit so it looks like shit. The finial's a faggot—a faggot hangs by his neck from the frame.

Fag-nifique!

The ballroom's a scene from some vampire Versailles. Count Choc-o-log's dancing with a dead faggot. Boo-Brownie and Franken-Fudge are disco-dancing together. Count Froufrou's dancing with Wolf-Wafer, a cartoon no one cares about. Wolf-Wafer's a faggot. Boo-Brownie's a faggot. Franken-Fudge's a faggot.

All faggots are cartoons.

Shit!

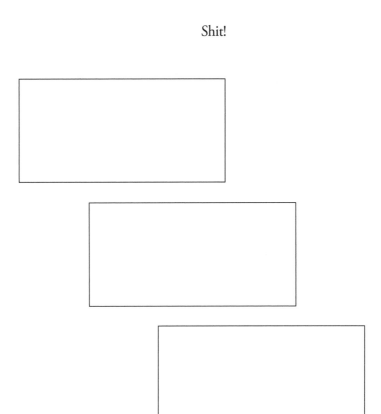

The crypt's beneath the ballroom. It's full of faggots. It's full of faggot suicides. It's full of faggot suicides' shit. The shit smells like faggot shit, like the stuff that faggots love to eat: shit, cum, and chocolate cereal.

Shit's the only food that looks the same going in as it looks coming out.

Why?

Why decorate a castle as a crypt?

For faggots, fucking's a form of decoration. What do you call a dick in an ass? Décor. What do you call shit in an ass? Décor.

What faggots did was to turn fucking into decorating. What faggots did was to turn decorating into fucking.

What's Castle Faggot? Imagine a castle that's been fucked. Imagine a castle that's been flipped ass-up and fucked. Imagine a castle that's been flipped ass-up so that crap from the crypt—the bats, the rats, the cocksucker corpses—drops down through the rooms and adorns them.

Who wants to live in a crypt?

A vampire.

A suicide.

At the end of Castle Faggot, there's the Castle Faggot
Gift Shop!

At the Castle Faggot Gift Shop, you can buy a dollhouse
of the castle. Faggots adore dollhouses. A dollhouse is décor
that contains décor. It's like if an asshole had its own asshole.
It's like if a shit could take a shit.

THE CASTLE FAGGOT DOLLHOUSE

Faggots!—come to Castle Faggot!

Faggots!—come to Castle Faggot and commit suicide!

For faggots who haven't come to the castle yet, and for faggots who've come but haven't committed suicide yet, there's this:

The Castle Faggot Dollhouse!

Walt Doody's Castle Faggot Dollhouse is the best thing besides being there. It lets you play with a dead faggot. It lets you play as a dead faggot. It lets you be a dead faggot—shove the castle up your ass and rupture your rectum.

If you can't die in the castle, die with the castle in you!

The Dollhouse

The Castle Faggot Dollhouse comes with:

■ A castle

The Décor

The Castle Faggot Dollhouse comes with décor:

■ A dead faggot
■ Bats and cobwebs
■ Skeletons and skulls
■ Shit

The dead faggot's a plastic figurine.

The bats and cobwebs are plastic bats and cobwebs. The skeletons and skulls are plastic skeletons and skulls.

The shit's actual shit.

The Design
The Castle Faggot Dollhouse comes with different rooms for you to decorate:

- A salon d'art
- A library
- A ballroom
- A crypt

The salon's in the tower. It's lined with paintings of Count Choc-o-log.
The paint's shit

The library's beneath it. It's lined with books about Count Choc-o-log and his buddies, Boo-Brownie and Franken-Fudge. The books are plastic.
The writing's shit.

The ballroom's beneath it. There are busts of the Count, Boo-Brownie and Franken-Fudge. The centerpiece's a crystal chandelier—it's plastic, clear plastic, so it looks like crystal. It's smeared with shit, so it looks like shit.

The crypt's smeared with shit.

Shit comes with the dollhouse. It's shit from faggots. For more shit, send a self-addressed stamped envelope to Shit c/o

Castle Faggot, or shove the castle up your ass and shit it yourself. If you're a boy who plays with dollhouses, you're already dead!

The Dolls

The Castle Faggot Dollhouse comes with dolls for you to play with:

- Count Choc-o-log
- Boo-Brownie
- Franken-Fudge
- Count Froufrou

Count Choc-o-log's a cartoon Dracula. He's the mascot of a chocolate cereal you faggots eat. It tastes like shit.

Boo-Brownie and Franken-Fudge are a cartoon ghost and ghoul. They're the mascots of their own cereals—Boo's is blue, Frank's is pink.

They taste like shit and dye.

Count Froufrou decorated the castle—he's an interior decorator to the undead. He's a cartoon of a faggot, a French faggot, a coprophagist, *n'est-ce pas?* He slicks his hair with shit. He slicks his moustache with shit. The stains on his teeth are shit—but only boys' shit.

Girls' shit is gross.

Count Froufrou's a cartoon of Count de Montesquiou,

The Count de Montesquiou was a faggot of fin-de-siècle France who was famous for his interior decoration.

The Count was a count. He had a castle in the countryside. He spent his time in an apartment in Paris. It was an attic apartment; he decorated it as a crypt. It had a walled-up window; it had a hall that led to a dead end; it had a gargantuan cobweb—gold thread stitched into red leather; it had bats—bisque bats, glass bats, more and more bats!

Moreau bats!

Why?

Why decorate an apartment as a castle's crypt?

Why be a fag? Why be French? As the French say:

"French French!"

The Dookydent Dolls

The Castle Faggot Dollhouse comes with more dolls for you to play with:

- Marcel Pooroust
- Jean Profitelorrain
- Charles Baudéclair
- Stéphane Marshmallarmé
- J.-Kouign-amann Huysmans

The Dookydents—that's what these dolls are called. They're faggots. They're writers—*quelle surprise*! Books they wrote line the library: *À rearbours* by Huysmans; *Les fleurs du malodeur* by Baudéclair; *À récherche du temps poo* by Pooroust.

As Marshmallarmé says in *Pooésies*: "*Amis, moi déjà sur la poop!*"

As Marshmallarmé says: "French French!"

Fin de siècle? Fag de siècle!

The Dookydents are cartoons of the Decadents.

The Decadents were faggot writers in fin-de-siècle France; they were famous for spreading Count de Montesquiou's style.

Stéphane Mallarmé described Montesquiou's décor in his diaries.

J.-K. Huysmans set his novel, *À rebours*, in Montesquiou's crypto-crypt; Montesquiou was the model for the dandy who dwells in it.

Marcel Proust put the crypto-crypt in his novel, *À la recherche du temps perdu*; the character of Baron de Charlus was based on Montesquiou. Jean Lorrain, too, put the crypto-crypt in his novel, *Monsieur de Phocas*; Montesquiou was the *monsieur*.

What are books?
Décor.
What are words?
French.
The Count de Montesquiou taught the Decadents about interior decoration.

The Count taught them to decorate as if they'd flipped a castle upside-down, so that crap from the crypt—the blood, the bones, the bodies—dropped down.

The Count taught them that death isn't a state—it's a style!

Marcel Proust kept his apartment as cold as a crypt. J.-K. Huysmans adorned his bedroom with monstrances. Jean Lorrain hung a beheaded head in his boudoir, blood dripping from its eyes and neck.

The blood was ribbons, the head bisque.

It was Belgian.

You can be a Decadent! Stick the Castle Faggot Dollhouse in your bedroom! Stick it up your ass—your ass is a dollhouse for shit!

Walt Doody
The Castle Faggot Dollhouse comes with another doll:

■ Walt Doody

Walt Doody looks like Walt Doody.

Walt Doody is the founder of Doodyland, the faggiest land in the world.

When Walt was a kid, his folks took him to the Kansas State Fair. He haunted the midway. He went through a haunted house.

A Trip to Hell, it was called.

There was Satan.

There were demons.

There were illusions: Man Turning to Skeleton, Man on Floor Minus His Head, Bottom of a Man With an Ass's Head, and the bloody Bluebeard's Castle:

"It contained seven heads," said Roltair, "made up as dead hung round the chamber on trays from which blood seemed to drip—the blood was aniline and it was supplied through rubber tubes."

Hell is a place decorated like Hell!

The illusions were the work of Henry Roltair.

Roltair was a mirror man. He made mirror boxes for magic shows. He made mirror illusions for sideshows. He made laughing mirrors for funhouses. He made mirror mazes for amusement parks and carnival companies.

The Roltair Mirror Manufactory operated out of a building on Broadway in New York. The first floor held a dime museum—exhibits by Roltair. The second story held a mirror maze—maze by Roltair. It led to his office, where he worked away on his masterpiece: The House Upside Down.

The House Upside Down had its debut at the World's Fair in Bismarck. It was remounted at the World's Fair in Omaha, then at the World's Fair in Milwaukee.

From Milwaukee, it went to France.

At the Exposition Universelle in Paris, Roltair recreated his "*maison à l'envers.*" It looked like it'd been upended. The roof sunk into the ground; the foundations stuck up into the sky. You entered through the attic and crossed the ceiling, sidestepping chandeliers that stood taller than you. You bumped your *tête* on chairs, tables, and lamps; open books like bats flying across the floor. You looked out the window and there was the Eiffel Tower—it, too, was upside-down.

It was mirrors. It was sideshow shit.

The Count de Montesquiou paid a visit to the inverted house. There he met Roltair, who fucked him up the ass.

Roltair, another faggot.

When Walt Doody went on A Trip to Hell, he shat his pants.

He decided that someday he'd build a ride that was smeared in shit—he was a fag and shit is faggy—all shit touches bums!

Where would he get so much shit? From suicides. Faggots were suicide machines. Suicides were shit machines. You take too many pills, you shit your pants. You slit your wrists, you shit your pants. You hang yourself, you shit your pants.

The faggot hanging in Castle Faggot got shit on the chandelier and on himself—his dick, his balls, his bobeche.

Asses are always upside-down.

RUE DU DOO
A Novelization

OOOOOOOOOOOOOOOOOOOOOOOOOOOOOOOOOOO
OOOOOOOOOOOOOOOOOOOOOOOOOOOOOOOOOO
OOOOOOOOOOOOOOOOOOOOOOOOOOOOOOOOOO
OOOOOOOOOOOOOOOOOOOOOOOOOOOOOOOOO
OOOOOOOOOOOOOOOOOOOOOOOOOOOOOOOOO
OOOOOOOOOOOOOOOOOOOOOOOOOOOOOOOOO
OOOOOOOOOOOOOOOOOOOOOOOOOOOOOOOOO
OOOOOOOOOOOOOOOOOOOOOOOOOOOOOOOOO
OOOOOOOOOOOOOOOOOOOOOOOOOOOOOOOOO
OOOOOOOOOOOOOOOOOOOOOOOOOOOOOOOOO
OOOOOOOOOOOOOOOOOOOOOOOOOOOOOOOOO
OOOOOOOOOOOOOOOOOOOOOOOOOOOOOOOOO
OOOOOOOOOOOOOOOOOOOOOOOOOOOOOOOOO
OOOOOOOOOOOOOOOOOOOOOOOOOOOOOOOOO
OOOOOOOOOOOOOOOOOOOOOOOOOOOOOOOOO
OOOOOOOOOOOOOOOOOOOOOOOOOOOOOOOOO
OOOOOOOOOOOOOOOOOOOOOOOOOOOOOOOOO
OOOOOOOOOOOOOOOOOOOOOOOOOOOOOOOOO
OOOOOOOOOOOOOOOOOOOOOOOOOOOOOOOOO
OOOOOOOOOOOOOOOOOOOOOOOOOOOOOOOOO
OOOOOOOOOOOOOOOOOOOOOOOOOOOOOOOOO
OOOOOOOOOOOOOOOOOOOOOOOOOOOOOOOOO
OOOOOOOOOOOOOOOOOOOOOOOOOOOOOOOOO
OOOOOOOOOOOOOOOOOOOOOOOOOOOOOOOOO
OOOOOOOOOOOOOOOOOOOOOOOOOOOOOOOOO
OOOOOOOOOOOOOOOOOOOOOOOOOOOOOOOOO
OOOOOOOOOOOOOOOOOOOOOOOOOOOOOOOOO
OOOOOOOOOOOOOOOOOOOOOOOOOOOOOOOOO
OOOOOOOOOOOOOOOOOOOOOOOOOOOOOOOOO
OOOOOOOOOOOOOOOOOOOOOOOOOOOOOOOOO
OOOOOOOOOOOOOOOOOOOOOOOOOOOOOOOOO

Intro

It's Paris, or a playset of Paris. A bat shits on cobblestones. The bat's a puppet. The shit's a puppet. Count Choc-o-log strolls down the street—he's a puppet. He sings:

"Somewhere beyond the box tops, here am I,

"I'm the Count from the breakfast cereal that you buy.

"Somewhere beyond the box tops, here I am,

"I'm the star of this special television program.

"Somewhere beyond the box tops, I am here,

"I'm in stop motion like Rudolph, the Red-Nosed Reindeer.

"Someday I'll slay that red-nosed clown and Santa, too, and flush them down the sewers. My show will air at Halloween and Christmastime and I'll be seen by billions of viewers!

"Somewhere beyond the box tops, here I'll be, way down deep in the—" He slips in shit. *"Shit! Shit is très, très Paris!"*

1.

"Die!" Count Choc-o-log chucks a shoe at a mirror. The mirror never sees it coming: the Count has no reflection; the Count's clothing has no reflection.

"Count Choc-o-log?" Boo-Brownie blows in.
"The mirror!" the Count says. "I hate the mirror!"
"You don't need a mirror," says Boo-Brownie, bobbing about like a blue balloon, or the ghost of a blue balloon. "You're perfect!"

"Friend?" Franken-Fudge clomps in.
"The Count's mad at the mirror," Boo-Brownie says.
"How can I see how fucking perfect I am," the Count says, "if I can't see how fucking perfect I am?"
"You no need mirror!" says Franken-Fudge, a pink Frankenstein. "You have friends. That suit suit you. Chocolate good color for Count!"

It's Castle Faggot. The ballroom. There's a bust of the Count. It's brown. There's a fancy chandelier. It's brown. There's a fancy mirror. It's broken in bits.

"What would you know-nothings know about it?" the Count says. "Ghosts can see themselves in mirrors—even though they're see-through! Monsters can see themselves— even though they're unsightly!"

"Things would be much clearer," the Count says, "and I'd be a chicer cerealier with a mirror, a mirror—a mirror!"

The Count sings:
"I could pick a pod of cocoa,
"I'd pin it to my coat so I'd have a boutonnière.
"I could wear a real bow tie and not a bat about to fly,
"If I only had a mirror."

The Count's bow tie flies off. It's brown. A brown bat.

"I could coif my coif up so high,
"I'd comb it up to the sky, or to the chandelier.
"I could wear Estée Lauder, put on lots of paint and powder,
"If I only had a mirror."

Boo-Brownie bobs about the chandelier. He holds bits of broken mirror in his hands: he's a *boo miroir.*

"Oh, me!" the Count sings. *"I'd like to see my* l'image inversée. *I'd look at myself and never look away. I'd look and look and look all day!*
"If I had a magic miroir,
"I'd slip into a peignoir, or something else that's sheer.
"À la Marie Antoinette, I'd see myself in my toilette,
"If I only had a mirror."

Cha-cha-cha—chocolate! Franken-Fudge disco dances across the brown broadloom. Dance doesn't describe it: heel to toe, heel to toe—he walks the way all stop motion animated puppets do, like he's learning to walk in high heels.

"*Alas!*" the Count sings as the music slows. "*I do not have a mirror because a mirror is a mere joke on a* vampyr."

"*A friend is a mirror with hair,*" Boo-Brownie sings.

"*Friend tell friend what to wear,*" Franken-Fudge sings.

"*A hairy mirror?*" the Count sings. "*Oh, dear, oh, dear, oh*—" He collapses like a push puppet, which he's not. The mirror's a puppet. It shattered in stop motion. The shoe's a puppet. Aren't all shoes puppets? Aren't all mirrors?

Franken-Fudge gives him some fudge.

"There's a mortal," Count Choc-o-log says, flinging the fudge aside, "a magical mortal, the most magical mortal of all. This wizard will make me a mirror, for there is nothing he cannot conjure. Shakespeare wrote of him, or Spenser, or someone—who gives a fuck? So long as he makes me a fucking mirror!"

The Count's bat comes back carrying the wizard. He doesn't look like a wizard. He's a boy with bad skin. And beady eyes. And a barrel chest.

I'm the boy. I'm not magical. The monsters don't know it yet.

I'm a puppet. I don't know it yet.

"I am Count Choc-o-log," the Count says, "the mascot of the breakfast cereal that bears my name."

My face is frightened.

The Count sings:

"Bienvenue au rue du Doo!"

Boo-Brownie and Franken-Fudge sing:

"*Tra-la-la, tra-la-la, tra-la-la-la-la-la-la!*"

"*From now on you'll be history,*" the Count sings, "*you'll be history, you'll be history! We'll glorify you every day! You'll be a bust in the mirror* musée!"

The Count:

"Boo-Brownie, welcome the wizard!"

"*I represent the Boo-Brownie brand,*" Boo-Brownie sings, "*the Boo-Brownie brand, the Boo-Brownie brand, and on behalf of the brand of Boo, I wish to welcome you to rue du Doo!*"

The Count:

"Franken-Fudge, do you have something to say?"

"*I am the Franken-Fudge friend for you,*" Franken-Fudge sings, "*friend for you, friend for you, and if you want to be friend of Frankie, too, I wish to welcome you to rue du Doo!*"

"Boo-Brownie and Franken-Fudge are cereal mascots, too," the Count says. "Boo-Brownie's cereal is blueberries and chocolate; Franken-Fudge's is strawberries and chocolate. They don't sell as well as mine. They look bad in the bowl—the toilet bowl! Boo-Brownie turns poo blue; Franken-Fudge turns poo pink.

"Count Choc-o-log," he says, "the cereal, is chocolate, and as such makes poo the darkest, dankest shade of brown—poopier than poop itself. It's poopy like a chocolate log, like a log inside the butt of a beautiful boy, like a beautiful log in the beautiful butt of—oh, but enough about my love life! Say something magical and mysterious!"

"Puppets!" I shrink away. "You're puppets! Puppets! Puppets! Puppets! Puppets! Puppets! Puppets! Puppets! Puppets! Puppets!"

Fade to brown, then fade in on—

I come to. I fainted before the fade. A puppet's in the room with me. He's dressed like a nineteenth-century French poet.

"Marshmallow?" I say.
"*Non*," he says, "I'm Marshmallarmé, Stéphane Marshmallarmé, a puppet and a poet, a poet and a puppet—a *poupoète*! You're a puppet, too."
"What do you mean?" My left eye falls off.
I shriek.

"Poopy?" I say.
"*Non*," he says, "I said *poupée*, it's a puppet *en français*."
"I'm a puppet in French?" My eye's plastique.
"Doodyland! You're a puppet in Doodyland! In Faggotland—it's the faggiest land in Doodyland!"

"Scary?" I say.
"Non," he says, "I said sucré, *les monstres sucrés*. The Count, Boo-Brownie, Franken-Fudge—all the mascots from monster cereals are here."

"They're not real!" I say.

My eye's a choking hazard.

"They're real *poupées*," he says. "Count Choc-o-log rules puppet Paris. He rules it with Bataille, who brought you into the store. Bataille is his bat. And his tie."

Bataille blows by.

"Count Choc-o-log lives here in Castle Faggot," he says. "He dines at Le Mâche-Merde. He shops at Le Mal Marché. It's the department store for puppet monsters. It's not Bergdorf Goodman, but Bergdorf Badman. It's on the rue du Doo."

Bataille takes a big shit.

"Besides being a poet, I am a fashion critic," Marshmallarmé says, shit on his shoulderpad. "I pen and publish a paper devoted to doings at Le Mal Marché—*La Dernière Mode*, I call it. The Count? What a wit. He calls it *La Derrière Mode*."

Marshmallarmé:

"I cover the Haunted Hair Salon," he says.

"Antoine is the salon's *chef coiffeur*.

"Franken-Fudge has his hair done there. He's a strawberry blond, but without the blond.

"Boo-Brownie has his hair blown out and dyed blue. Sometimes he wears bangs, a bob or a bouffant. He always wears a boater.

"Hair's dead matter. Hair's the corpse of hair. The Count's worn the same style always—hair piled into a peak, like a Dairy Queen dipped cone, or a Hershey kiss."

"How does it stay up?" I say.
"Chocolate mousse."

"I cover the Haunted Cosmetics Counter," he says.
"Choclette is the counter's *chef cosméticienne.*
"Franken-Fudge doesn't need blush, but he wears it anyway. His head's a strawberry. He has seeds.
"Boo-Brownie's bonkers for blue eye shadow. He looks like he's made of blue eye shadow; like he's the ghost of blue eye shadow.
"People expire; cosmetics do, too. Monsters wear makeup that's gone bad. Testers teem with germs. After a vampire's used your lip gloss, it's garbage. The Count prefers an evening palette—brown."

"Who makes monster makeup?" I say.
"Cover Ghoul."

"I cover the Haunted Couture Atelier," he says.
"Franken-Fudge will wear anything pink.
"Boo-Brownie's a ghost in a blue shirt. He's the ghost of a blue shirt. What size shirt does a spiritualist wear? Medium.
"Cocoa Chanel sews suits for the Count. He wears her exclusively. She's more than his seamstress: she's his screamstress.

"Like all vampires, he can become a bat. When he changes into a bat, his suit must shrink to size. When he changes back, his suit must change back, too. The cloth's woven from vampire bat fur. And a lot of elastic."

"Who sews Boo-Brownie's shirt?" I say.
"Boo-lenciaga!"

"The Count lives in Castle Faggot," he says. "He prays at Sucre Coeur Cathedral—it's *sucrelège*! He's despicable—contemptful of his fellow monster mascots. Contemptful of the staff at Le Mal Marché—his *coiffeur*, his *cosméticienne* and his *couturière*. He reserves his cruelest contempt for the children that consume his cereal. He murders boys. He loves to murder boys. He's the most murderous cereal mascot since Gilles de Raisin.

"He didn't murder you yet," he says to me. "*Pourquoi pas?*"

"Wizard!"
Count Choc-o-log comes into the scene and sings:
"*I'm here to see the wizard, this wonderful wizard of ours.*
"*I hear he is a wonderful wiz with wonderful wizard powers.*"
With Boo-Brownie and Franken-Fudge behind him, bopping to the beat, the Count continues his tune:
"*I hear this wiz is* fantastique, *he'll make me a* miroir magique, *because, because, because, because, because—I have the gall of a* Gauloise!"
"You're awake, wizard," the Count says.
"Wizard?" I say. "I'm Derek. Derek McCormack."

"Derek McCormack?" the Count says. "That's not your name. Your real name is John Dee."

"My name's Jonathon Derek McCormack," I say. "I'm from Peterborough. I go to Peterborough Civic High School. Mom and Dad call me Jon-D. My teachers call me Derek. My classmates call me fudge-packer. Or fruitcake. Or faggot. Or fag."

"That's some wizard," Boo-Brownie snickers.
"I like Snickers!" Franken-Fudge says.

"You're John Dee!" the Count says. "You're the great wizard!"

"No!" I say.

"No? No one says no to me!"

"I'm sorry, but you're mistaken."

"Mistaken? I don't make mistakes!"

"I don't know anything about being a wizard. I've played Wizard, the board game. I own Merlin, the Electronic Wizard. I've eaten Alpha-Bits—there's a wizard on Alpha-Bits, isn't there?"

"Wizard, you will make me a magic mirror so that I may see myself reflected!" He rises off the rug. His strings are almost see-through. "And if you don't, then I will eat you for breakfast and shit you out before lunch!"

Wipe to—

"Boys eat Count Choc-o-log," Marshmallarmé says. "Count Choc-o-log eats boys."

I shake because I'm scared, and because a puppeteer's making me shake.

It's me and Marshmallarmé in the scene.

"Sugar," he says.
From his pocket he pulls a palmful of cereal.
It's Count Choc-o-log. I pop some in my mouth.
"Count Choc-o-log cereal's sugar—brown O's and bits of brown marshmallow, or marbits.
"It's beloved by children and also by adolescents with poor palates. It makes children obese and diabetic and it decays their teeth—and it does worse things, as well."

"Shit," he says.
He scoops up some of Bataille's shit.
It's Count Choc-o-log. I gag on what I'm chewing.
"Count Choc-o-log cereal's shit— brown O's and bits of brown marshmallow, or marbits.
"The Count captures boys who eat his cereal and spirits them back to his puppet world. Bats devour them, then defecate. The Count boxes the bung, then sells it as Count Choc-o-log. The cereal's sugary, so the boys are sugary, so the cereal's sugary, so the boys are sugary, and so on."

Marshmallarmé sings:
"Snap, snap, snap!
"Crackle, crackle, crack!

"Poop, poop, poop, poo!

"That's how bats bake up breakfast, boy, on the scary old rue du Doo.

"Cric, cric, cric!

"Crac, crac, crac!

"Caca, the grossest goût!

"A bowlful or a bowel full, bon appetit au *rue du Doo."*

"Toddlers, teens, in-betweens," he says. "The Count's butchered countless boys. What could I do to deter him? I'm a fashion critic. I'm a poet. A *poète maudit.*

"A *poète* marbit!

"I can't protect all boys from the Count, but perhaps I can protect you. If he wants you to be a wizard, then you'll be a wizard. He'll have his mirror, I'll make sure of—"

"Wizard!" Cocoa Chanel comes into the room.

"A-ha-ha-ha!" Choclette comes in, cackling. Her hair stands on end. Her hair's made from a white makeup brush. It's weasel.

"Well, well, well, if it isn't the wiz!" Antoine comes in. White suit, white shirt, white wig. White wig glue drips down the sides of his head. It will not yellow. He tosses white confetti at me.

"What do you want?" I say.

"The Count's my best customer!" Antoine says. "He comes to my salon every day, sometimes several times a day, to have his hair blown out and brushed. He comes because he can't do it himself. Because he can't see himself in mirrors. If you make a mirror for the Count, how will I make a living, or a dying? Who would be my best customer? Wolf-Wafer? He only has hair on a full moon!"

"Wolf-Wafer wanted me to make him a fur coat," Cocoa Chanel says, "to cover his hide when he wasn't furry. I did. He brought it back. He was covered in boils. I knew he was averse to silver, but even to silver fox?"

"When you pierce Wolf-Wafer's ears, don't put in silver studs," Choclette says. "I found that out the hard way."

Laughter from nowhere.

Antoine:

"I learned my art by dressing my dear mother's hair. It was the old days—I'd pin it up and decorate it with hair pieces and hair pins and jewelry and then I'd perfume it.
"Mother was my masterpiece. I was taken on by the most prestigious hair salon in all of Paris. I'd rise with the sun, then do mother's do, then walk to work, which was on the Champs Elysées. The day she died, I was late leaving for the salon, I didn't have time to do her hair, I swore to her that I would do it later on.

"Heartbroken, I was heartbroken! I buried her with her white, white hair spilling across her white, white pillow. I returned to the salon and continued to coif hair for the finest *femmes* in Paris—that is, until I happened to see a piece in a newspaper, a scientist saying that a corpse's hair continues to grow even in the grave. I dashed to the graveyard. I dug her up.

"Could you die? Her hair was a horror. I washed and brushed it and put it up in a bun. I did this every night for weeks. I became concerned about other corpses, women strewn throughout the cemetery, without sons to tend to their hair. I dug up other mothers, I styled their locks. Ghoul! This is what a guard said to me when he discovered me one evening. He swung a shovel at my skull. I died. I will not let you take away the Count! I will die a thousand more times before I allow you to do that!"

"A-ha-ha-ha!" Choclette cackles.

"Cosmetics are my specialty. I made myself up—pretty, yes?" Her eyebrows are drawn on; her eyelashes, Dacron.

"The Count comes to my counter every day, since he can't apply his own cosmetics. He'd put lipstick on his eyebrows and pencil on his nose!" She has brown lipstick on her teeth. I think it's lipstick.

"If you make him a magic mirror, he'll need me no more. If he doesn't need me anymore, then you, wizard—" She points a big brown fingernail at me. The brown is nail polish. I think. "—will wind up like Fang, my dear departed hubby, may he rest in pain. A-ha-ha-ha!"

Choclette:

"Fang had a funeral home. He'd drain and disembowel the bodies; I'd make-up them so that they looked the way they did when they were alive.

"White wax for filling in cuts and hollows; skin-tone cream for concealing bruises and scars; rouge for reddening the lips and cheeks, and powder to set it—these were the tools of the trade. With them, I turned stiffs into stars and starlets, at least for a couple hours.

"'None of them is as beautiful as you, Choclette!' That's what my Fang would say to me.

"I used a little of the mortician make-up myself. The lipstick was packed with dye so it was almost permanent; I'd put it on before bed. It'd last the night, no matter what the hubby and I happened to get up to! Then the hubby stopped getting up to anything with me—he was sneaking around behind my back. With a widow!

"A-ha-ha-ha! I did what any woman would do—I strapped him to the draining table, stuck cotton up his ass, cotton soaked in phenol. I pumped embalming fluid into his artery—formaldehyde dyed pink, to give him some color. The screams! He screamed until I stitched his lips shut. He was embalmed before he died! The judge and jury did not find it funny. I hanged for it. But I still have Fang. After I died, I dug him up. He's on the sofa. He's a bolster. A-ha-ha-ha!"

"I still have Mother's hair!" Antoine says. "I wove it into a wig!" He lifts his wig. A snake crawls from a crack in his skull. A snake, then a spider, then a millipede, then an ant.

His head's a Thingmaker.

"Wizard!" Cocoa Chanel says, "I don't know what magical powers you possess. For your sake, I hope they are formidable.

"If I were you, I'd magically remove myself from rue du Doo immediately," she says, circling me. "The Count doesn't need your mirror; I will not allow a mirror to be made.

"I'm the Count's mirror. I, too, am magic; this is my wand." From her hair she pulls a hatpin. Her hair is pulled back in a bun, or brioche. She's gray. So's her skin. Her dress is chocolate crêpe. "It grants me mastery over life and death—well, mostly death."

Cocoa Chanel:

"I lost my daughter.

"I was a poor dressmaker, and she was struck with typhus. What could I do?

"While I sewed gowns for the wealthiest women in Paris, she lay in her bed, dying, dying—and then she was dead.

"Silk, satin, velvet—all day I created confections from fine fabrics brought to me by my clients, and yet I buried her in a shroud made from her bedsheets. God forgive me, I couldn't afford anything else!

"I was sewing in my small room when she came back to me, appearing in her spectral form.

"'Mother,' she said, 'I am well, the afterworld is wonderful, it's like a wonderful party full of wonderful people, but there is something about it I do not like: I'm doomed to wear this for all eternity!'

"So I stole. I stole yards of satin, I stole yards of silk. I stole them from my customers' stock—they wouldn't notice, they had cloth to spare. I made for my daughter the grandest gown, so frilly, so flouncy.

"While the city slept, I dug up her corpse and dressed her in her party frock. I didn't disinter her alone, of course; I couldn't shovel all that soil. I was assisted by a strange man, a ghoul. I encountered him at the cemetery. While I drew the dress up around her bones, he dressed her hair."

"Hello, Frisco!" Antoine says, flinging confetti.

"I was in my small sewing studio when again she returned to me, appearing in her spectral form. She still wore her shroud.

"'Darling daughter, I said, why aren't you wearing the gorgeous gown that I created for you? Don't you like it?'

"'Mother, I can't wear it!' she said. "I'm dead, but the dress isn't. When the Grim Reaper came for me, he cut me down with his scythe; he also cut down the bedsheets I was wrapped in. I'm dead, the sheets are dead, but the dress isn't. The dress must die.'

"In the dead of night I returned to the cemetery. Assisted by Antoine, I disintered my daughter for the second time. I undressed her. I held the dress I had made, the beautiful dress—and I stabbed it. I stabbed it through the breast with a butcher's knife.

(57)

"'Oh, mother, I adore it!' my dear daughter said when she materialized before me in my sewing studio. 'It's the dress I dreamed of owning when I was alive!' She was wearing the dress I had murdered for her; she was a ghost in the ghost of a dress.

"'Thanks to my dress,' my daughter said, 'I have become the belle of the by-and-by. All the dead ladies want to try it on. All the dead gentlemen want to walk with me through Elysium.' As she spoke, I wept, for all I ever wanted was for her to be fashionable. 'Dying is not so dire, Mother, not when a spectre has such a wonderful wardrobe!'

"I went to work. I made her dresses for day, then stabbed them. I made her evening gowns, then poured poison on them. I made her coats and capes, then doused them with benzene and burned them. I used the fabric that my clients had purchased for me. When my clients came calling, I refused to come to the door.

"The police came. I climbed out the window.

"I fled first to Le Printemps, the department store. I swept along the aisles, stabbing a hatpin in hats, gloves and purses. I stabbed dresses, too. The clerks in the store attempted to apprehend me; I eluded them. I fled to Galeries Lafayette. Sweaters, skirts, scarves and shoes—my slaughter of fine clothes continued.

"The police came for me there. I slipped into the street.

"The Opéra! It was close to curtain time. Paris's most fashionable femmes were pouring into the foyer. I saw the finest dresses I had ever seen. The cuts! The colors! I saw a Paul Poiret. I stabbed it until it died a death. I saw a Charles Frederick Worth of black bombazine. I stabbed it. I stabbed a Callot Soeurs, a Vionnet, a Fortuny. Too bad for the ladies wearing them—I stabbed them, too. Then I tore off a long strip of my dress and swallowed it. I suffocated. With my daughter is where I belong! With the demons of Rue du Doo! With the Count!"

Antoine sings:
"Snip, snip here,
"Clip, clip there.
"I put poo in shampoo.
"I'll put you in the grave, John Dee,
"On the scary old rue du Doo."

Choclette sings:
"Lash, lash here,
"Lips, lips there.
"John Dee's a parvenu.
"I'll put cosmetics on his corpse,
"On the scary old rue Du Doo."

Cocoa Chanel sings:
"Stitch, stitch here,
"Stitch, stitch there.
"Some couture, Count, pour vous—
"I sewed it from the wizard's skin,
"On the scary old rue du Doo."

The puppets laugh and leave.

Cut to commercial.

"What will I do, Marshmallarmé?" I say. "I'm dead if I don't make a mirror, and I'm dead if I do!"

"Welcome to the show," Marshmallarmé says.
"Show?" I stare into the camera.
"*Rue du Doo*. The show you're in. The show we're in. It's playing on Channel 12. It's 7:30 pm."

"Do you know *Rudolph, the Red-Nosed Reindeer*?" he says.
I nod, or someone makes me nod.
"*Rudolph* was also a stop motion tv special. Rankin/Bass, the puppeteers, made it.

"*Rudolph* had a misfit reindeer; *Rue du Doo* has a misfit boy—you! You're a tv star. It's Rudolph on the Rue du Doo. It's Rue-du-doo-dolph."

"*Rudolph, the Red-Nosed Reindeer* was the first successful stop motion tv special," he says. "*Rue du Doo* follows its formula."
I blink. It makes a blinking sound.
"Rankin/Bass made the *Rudolph* puppets by hand, then animated them in Japan. Johnny Marks wrote Christmas songs for them to sing.

"*Rue du Doo* is more rank than Rankin, more ass than Bass. The songs are about poop. Rip Taylor is the voice of Antoine. Phyllis Diller is the voice of Choclette. Jonathan Winters is Cocoa Chanel. Paul Lynde plays Ploppy, a poo."

"Who does my voice?" I say.

"A girl," he says.

"*Rudolph, the Red-Nosed Reindeer* was a Christmas special; it was an ad for the idea of Christmas.

"*Rue du Doo*'s an ad for faggots.

"*Rudolph* premiered on the Fantasy Hour. It was sponsored by General Electric. It was good advertising for GE and for all the gadgets they sold as Christmas gifts: a steam iron, a can opener, an electric knife. *Rue du Doo*'s part of Walt Doody's weekly series. It's sponsored by Doodyland and by Count Choc-o-log, of course.

"Shit, sponsored by sugar!"

"I don't know a thing about acting!" I say.

"Acting?" he says.

"You're here to sell cereal; you're here to sell toys.

"You're here to sell the Count figurine, the Boo-Brownie figurine, the Franken-Fudge figurine—yours for five boxtops and a money order.

"You're here to sell the Haunted Mirror playset, with shattering mirror. The mirror's foil. The Count's foiled by it! You're here to sell the Haunted Hair Salon, the Haunted Cosmetics Counter, the Haunted Haute Couture Atelier—yours for twenty-five box tops and a money order, sets sold separately.

"Then there's this."

He holds up a dollhouse.

"It's Barbie's dream house, but built for Barbey D'Aurevilly!"

It's plastic—a plastic castle.

"The Castle Faggot Dollhouse, yours for fifty boxtops and a money order. For faggots age five and up."

I peer into it. I see me: a figurine of me in it. The figurine's peering into a doll-sized dollhouse that a figurine of Marshmallarmé has in his hands.

"It doesn't belong on a table." Marshmallarmé holds it upside-down. "It's made to be mounted upside-down under a table. Cereal boxes and bowls sit on tables; the dollhouse belongs to the world beneath the bowls and boxes; the dark underworld where the cereal in the boxes and bowls is made, made and made into *merde*. Mouths may gobble up Count Choc-o-log, but this is where the gobblings go—below, below, below."

2.

All alone in the Castle Faggot
Dollhouse, I sing:

"*Somewhere beyond the box tops, brown
bats fly,*

"*Bats that poop puppet poop on Paris and
on Versailles.*

"*Somewhere beyond the box tops, brown
bats soar,*

"*Bats that poop in a monster puppet
department store.*

"*Somewhere beyond the box tops, bats
brought me,*

"*And I'm trapped in a world of stop
motion puppetry.*

"*Someday I'll wake up with a scream,
someday I'll wake from this bad dream called
Paree.*

"*I'll eat fresh fruit and Wheaties, too,
not cereal made of bat poo and dingleberry!*

"*Somewhere beyond the box tops, bats
fly free,*" I sing, tears falling at twenty-four
frames a second, "*bats fly beyond the box
tops, but what of, what of—me?*"

Applause.

A puppet applauds me. "What a lovely song," he says.

"Really?" I say, sniffling.

"No! It was so faggy! You're fagging up the whole store!" He grins. Giggles. Guffaws. He's my age, but gorgeous. Big brown eyes in a big round head. And his bum—it's as if another puppet head's been stuffed down the back of his pants.

He winks, then he's gone.

I have a hard-on. It's plastic wood. It took ten puppeteers ten minutes to animate it. Why?

Wipe to—

"*Somewhere beyond the box tops,*" I sing, "*I dream of a beautiful boy—is it puppy or puppet love?*"

"A saccharine sentiment."

I didn't see Marshmallarmé come in.

"Who is this wonderful boy who's inspired you to sing?" he says.

"I don't know his name," I say. "He dropped by the room. He was really cute. Really, really cute. Really, really, really cute!"

"*Merde*," he mutters to himself.

"The mirror," he says. "If you want to live, you must make the magic mirror and make it immediately!" He hands me a book, a big book. "You are no longer Jon-D; you are John Dee."

"Wizard!" the Count says, strutting into the scene with Boo-Brownie and Franken-Fudge. "Where's my magic mirror? Is this crackpot poet preventing you from completing it?"

"Count," Marshmallarmé says, "I'm here in my capacity as a reporter. I'm planning on profiling the wizard in an upcoming edition of *La Dernière Mode*."

"*La Derrière Mode*," the Count sneers.

"The wizard was showing me the book he wrote—weren't you, wizard?"

Marshmallarmé nudges me and I nod.

"It includes incantations to conjure the archangel Anael, who governs Venus, the planet, and who oversees the forces of love and hate in this world."

"Anal," the Count sneers.

"Anael's armed with the secrets of reflection, and of foreseeing the future in shiny surfaces—isn't he, wizard?"

Marshmallarmé nudges me and I nod.

"It'll take the wizard some time to summon the archangel and study his secrets so that he can create a magic mirror capable of reflecting a vampire puppet. He'll need privacy, absolute privacy, so shall we all leave him alone to—Count?"

"Arthur!" the Count says, spinning around. "I smell him!"

The Count sings:

"*Come out, come out, wherever you are, and meet the wise wizard who fell from a star.*

"*Come out, come out, wherever you be, and meet the wise wizard who's known as John Dee.*

"*Come out, come out, wherever thou art, and*—oh, for fuck's sake," he says, ditching the good witch demeanor. "Arthur, you little shit, come out! Come out or so help me God!"

"Arthur?" I say.

"Arthur Rainblo!" the Count says. "He's a punk! He's a prankster! He's a pain in my ass! When I get my hands on him I am going to murder him! But before I murder him, I'm going to fuck the shit out of him!"

"Fist him!" Boo-Brownie says.
"Felch him!" Franken-Fudge says.

"Arthur Rainblo's a brat, you see; but he's also the most succulent creature in *tout* Paris, the faggot dream of the *fin de fudgesicle*!" the Count says, silly strings of spittle dangling from his fangs. "He's a boy made of chocolate—chocolate hair, chocolate eyes, and a big beautiful butt full of brown!"

"I would hold it dear," the Count says, "I'd slobber, slurp and smear his rear, his rear—his rear!"

The Count sings:

"Arthur's ass is a confection,

"That gives me an erection, so let me make it clear,

"I would pig out on a plate of that guy's gorgeous chocolate,

"If I only had his rear."

The Count dances across the room.

"Arthur's ass is chocolate candy,

"And chocolate makes me randy and fills me with désir.

"Watch me sink my dent sucrée *deep in his dark dessert buffet,*

"If I only had his rear."

The Count dances up the wall. He dances across the ceiling. Fred Astaire? Fred Ascare!

"Sweet meat! I'd like to eat his plump posterior. I'd eat it a while and then eat it some more. I bet it's better than a S'more!

"If I devoured his derrière,

"His seductive sucrière, *his cheeky chocolatier,*

"I could blame my tooth decay on Arthur's rectal cavité,

"If I only had his rear."

"Alas, I do not have his rear," he sings as the music slows, *"and I never will, I fear—I shed the sweetest tear. A candy store in a kid is how I'd satisfy my id, if I only had his rear."*

He sheds a tear. It's cellophane. It's a candy wrapper.

Rue du Doo will be right back.

"'After my fervent prayers made to God, for his mercifull comfort and instruction, throwgh ministery of his holy and myghty powers did he dyspatch to me an Angel, named Anael, yf it were his divine pleasure ….'"

I read John Dee. I revise John Dee:

"'After my fervent prayers made to
God, for his mercifull comfort and instruction, throwgh ministery of his holy and
myghty powers did he dyspatch to me an
Angel, named Arthur, yf it were his divine
pleasure .... '"

Arthur appears.

"Wizard!"
I drop the book.
"What the hell are you doing?" he says.
"Why are you reading some stupid book?"
"The Count—"
"Fuck the Count! The Count thinks he
can make you do whatever he wants. He
thinks he can make us all do whatever he
wants.

"There's only one way to deal with the
Count: cruelly. The crueler I am to him,
the more he loves me; the more he loves
me, the more he wants to murder me.
Also—I have an awesome ass!"

"I'll show you," he says with a smile,
"what a badass I can be."

Wipe to—

"Arthur!"

The Count dashes into the room.

"Arthur Rainblo?" I say. "He's not here."

"My fangs! My fearsome fangs!" He's fangless. "I fell asleep for the day and the little puke pulled them out!"

He shoves wax fangs into his mouth.

"What kind of vampire wears wax fangs? What kind of demon wears dentures? What kind—" He coughs. He gags. He swallows his fangs, or they swallow him.

Wipe to—

"Where is he?"

The Count dashes into the room.

"Where's who?" I say.

"You know damned well who!"

"What did Arthur do?"

"What does it look like he did? He dropped water balloons on me—but it wasn't water, it was milk!" Milk makes his makeup run. Milk makes his hair dye drip. "I'm melting!"

A bunch of brown puddles behind him, milk and whatever he's made of—BHT, Blue 1, Yellow 6, Red 40.

Wipe to—

"I'm Christmas!"

The Count comes into the room.

"I'm fucking Christmas!"

The Count's head is his head, but it's not on his body.

"Santa?" I say.

"I'm Count fucking Claus!" The Count's head's been stuck to Santa's body. "I'm a piece-of-shit puppet from *Rudolph, the Red-Nosed Reindeer!*"

"I love that show."

"It's the dumbest damned special that Rankin/Bass made!" The Count's head is stuck on with grade-school glue. Which crusts. Which creeps. Which is built up like a beard beneath his chin. The Count's head comes off. It lands upside-down by Santa's boots. "You're dead, Arthur!" the Count's head says. "You're deader than dead!"

Wipe to—

"Ha!

"Ha! Ha!

"Ha! Ha! Ha!

Arthur rolling on the rug.

"Aren't you scared?" I say, getting down on the rug beside him.

"The Count's not scary!" he says. "He's a bumbling boob. He's a Bumble! I'm Hermey! You're Rudolph, the fucking reindeer!"

Arthur comes close.

"You're the star of the show. You'll win out in the end, but not before you meet some monsters, suffer some scares, escape from some scrapes. You'll sing some songs. You'll make friends. You'll have some romance."

Arthur kisses me.

"Arthur!" I say, shying away.

"You're cute," he says.

"No, I'm not!"

"You're faggy and funny-looking. I think that's cute."

"You're Arthur Rainblo! You should
have your own cereal! You should have
your own puppetoon!"

He puts my hand down his pants. His
ass is soft. Soft-touch vinyl.

My eyes are decals of mouths.

Arthur takes off his t-shirt.
My clothes are glued to my body.
Arthur takes off his trousers. He pulls
apart his cheeks. The asshole's like a mold
for making asshole-shaped sweets.

I lick it. It puckers like my tongue is
tart.

He reaches back and forces my face in
further. My tongue's tiny. It's a tasting
spoon. What's on it? Sauce. Sauce like on a
sundae—chocolatey and hot. It oozes into
my mouth and onto my lips. It slides down
my chin and coats my cheeks. It smears
across my eyes and brow and eyebrows.
Eyebrowns. Where's the cherry? Where are
the nuts?

I know where are the nuts.

"You should see yourself," he laughs when I'm full of his fudge. "You look like my ass!"

Wipe to—

"Why?
"Why do I care?
"Why do I worry?"
Marshmallarmé storms around the room:
"John Dee's book has been here for days and you've barely cracked it.

"Do you not realize the seriousness of this situation? Do you not comprehend what the Count will do to you? Do you not understand that you will die and die in a dreadful—"

"A brown mirror," I say.

"What was that?" Marshmallarmé says.
"A brown mirror," I say, "is what the Count needs."
"Derek, you did it!" He's animated. "I doubted you, but you did it—a brown mirror is precisely what the Count requires!"

"You knew?"

"Of course! I was waiting for you to discover it for yourself. I needed you to discover it for yourself in the John Dee book, so that this damned special could redeem itself with a moral: Reading is important!"

"I didn't read the book," I say. "It was Arthur's ass. I was brown and it was brown. Brown's a mirror for brown!"

"The ass is an abyss," Marshmallarmé says, addressing the audience directly:

"A mirror is the devil's ass.

"*Speculum fallax*—this is what philosophers call convex mirrors, for such mirrors distort the world as the devil does.

"And convex mirrors are bulbous, like the best butts."

"John Dee didn't just have a convex mirror. He had a black convex mirror.

"It was even eviler.

"The mirror meant he could capture demons.

"Catoptromancy—it's what Dee did. He summoned the demons in his mirror. The demons foretold famines, catastrophes, plagues. He spoke to the devil's ass and it spoke to him!

"Arthur's ass is Dee's malevolent mirror made flesh and farts. It's full of BM— brown magic!

"The Count's black mirror will be brown. It will consist of a convex mirror in the shape of Arthur's ass, with a coat of brown paint as a tain."

"Arthur has a taint!" I say.

"John Dee practiced black arts in black mirror," he says. "The Count will practice his brown arts in a brown mirror. He will watch it like it's a brown tv and he's always on every station!"

Wipe to—

The Count sings to me:
"I thank you very sweetly,
"For showing me completely,
"Myself from head to feetly,
"So I thank you very sweetly!"

"Glamorous!" the Count says.

"Gorgeous!" he says.

"Groovy!" he says.

The mirror's curved like the bottom of a creme egg. The mirror's the color of a creme egg. The Count is admiring himself in it. Boo-Brownie and Franken-Fudge are admiring the Count as he admires himself in it.

"In honor of of this magical mirror that you created," the Count says, "I shall send you back to the world from which you came!"

"No," I say.

"No?" he says.

"No?" Marshmallarmé says.

"I have fallen in love!" I say. "I have fallen in love with Faggotland. I have fallen in love with Castle Faggot. I have fallen in love with a boy! With your consent, Count, I'd like to stay and become a citizen of puppet Paris—*un Pouparisien!*"

Wipe to—

"*Somewhere beyond the box tops,*" I sing, "*I am hearts for a boy who poos chocolate poos and farts chocolate farts.*"

Marshmallarmé storms in.

"Have you lost your mind?" he says. "This isn't your world!"

"Arthur's ass is my world!" I say.

"There are those who do not want you here," he says. "Have you forgotten that? Have you forgotten about—"

Antoine, Choclette and Cocoa Chanel—they come in together.

"Wizard!" Antoine says.

"We warned you!" Choclette says.

"We told you not to make the Count a mirror!" Cocoa Chanel says. "We told you that there would be consequences!"

"I did it for Arthur!" I say.

"Ha!" Cocoa Chanel says. "Don't mention that stupid little shit to me. If he had done what he was supposed to do, that mirror would still be a mad dream in the Count's mind."

"What?" I say.

"Arthur doesn't give a crap about you. I hired him to distract you. I hired him to distract you from the work that you were supposed to be doing. He didn't do a very damned good job of it, did he?"

"What?" I say.

"Oh, I'm sorry, did I hurt you?" she says. "Did I hear your heart break? Choclette! The wizard is heartbroken!" Choclette blows smoke in my face. She has a cigarette holder as long as her nose. Theater length. "Antoine! The wizard believed that a boy like Arthur could like him!"

Antoine tosses confetti in my face.

"Show business!" he says.

Wipe to—

I'm curled up in a corner.

"Ooh, it's the magical wizard!" Arthur says as he comes in. "What the hell were you thinking? You weren't supposed to make that mirror! You were supposed to fall for me!"

"I did fall for you!"

"Well, you shouldn't have! Cocoa Chanel protects me from the Count. She said to distract you and so I did. You were having fun, I was having fun. Then you went and wrecked it all.

"The Count hates me, Cocoa Chanel hates me—where the hell am I going to go? What am I going to do? I'll have to sail away with Cap'n Crunch on the S.S. Guppy. I'll have to flee to Africa with Toucan Sam. Say so long to this—you'll never taste it again!"

He bends over to show me his behind.

I grab the big book of John Dee.

I bring it down on his head.

Fade to brown, then fade in on—

The Count and I stand side by side
before Arthur, who's hanging from the
chandelier. He's hanging from chains. The
Count chained him up.

"No!" Arthur says.

"Derek, don't do this!" he says.
"You love me!" he says.
"You said—"
A bat flies into his ass. It tears straight
through his body and comes out his crotch.
Arthur bleeds fake blood. It's not fake to
him.

Bats, bats, bats—brown bats careen
down from the ceiling. A bat tears through
his neck. A bat tears into his face, then out
the back of his skull. A bat tears into his
chest, cracking his ribs, cracking his spine,
then comes out the other side.
He's dead. He's like a shape sorter with
only one shape: bat.

The bats flock back to the ceiling, flocking it with fur. They hang upside-down like dollhouses.

They shit. They shit on his body. They shit on his blood, which is syrup. The blood has a skin. They shit in the Count's mouth, which is hinged. They shit on my tongue, which I'm sticking out.

I have shit in my hair. I have shit on my collar. I'm up to my knees in Count Choc-o-log.

What it's like to be a premium.

OOOOOOOOOOOOOOOOOOOOOOOOOOOOOOOOOO
OOOOOOOOOOOOOOOOOOOOOOOOOOOOOOOOOO
OOOOOOOOOOOOOOOOOOOOOOOOOOOOOOOOOO
OOOOOOOOOOOOOOOOOOOOOOOOOOOOOOOOOO
OOOOOOOOOOOOOOOOOOOOOOOOOOOOOOOOOO
OOOOOOOOOOOOOOOOOOOOOOOOOOOOOOOOOO
OOOOOOOOOOOOOOOOOOOOOOOOOOOOOOOOOO
OOOOOOOOOOOOOOOOOOOOOOOOOOOOOOOOOO
OOOOOOOOOOOOOOOOOOOOOOOOOOOOOOOOOO
OOOOOOOOOOOOOOOOOOOOOOOOOOOOOOOOOO
OOOOOOOOOOOOOOOOOOOOOOOOOOOOOOOOOO
OOOOOOOOOOOOOOOOOOOOOOOOOOOOOOOOOO
OOOOOOOOOOOOOOOOOOOOOOOOOOOOOOOOOO
OOOOOOOOOOOOOOOOOOOOOOOOOOOOOOOOOO
OOOOOOOOOOOOOOOOOOOOOOOOOOOOOOOOOO
OOOOOOOOOOOOOOOOOOOOOOOOOOOOOOOOOO
OOOOOOOOOOOOOOOOOOOOOOOOOOOOOOOOOO
OOOOOOOOOOOOOOOOOOOOOOOOOOOOOOOOOO
OOOOOOOOOOOOOOOOOOOOOOOOOOOOOOOOOO
OOOOOOOOOOOOOOOOOOOOOOOOOOOOOOOOOO
OOOOOOOOOOOOOOOOOOOOOOOOOOOOOOOOOO
OOOOOOOOOOOOOOOOOOOOOOOOOOOOOOOOOO
OOOOOOOOOOOOOOOOOOOOOOOOOOOOOOOOOO
OOOOOOOOOOOOOOOOOOOOOOOOOOOOOOOOOO
OOOOOOOOOOOOOOOOOOOOOOOOOOOOOOOOOO
OOOOOOOOOOOOOOOOOOOOOOOOOOOOOOOOOO
OOOOOOOOOOOOOOOOOOOOOOOOOOOOOOOOOO
OOOOOOOOOOOOOOOOOOOOOOOOOOOOOOOOOO
OOOOOOOOOOOOOOOOOOOOOOOOOOOOOOOOOO
OOOOOOOOOOOOOOOOOOOOOOOOOOOOOOOOOO
OOOOOOOOOOOOOOOOOOOOOOOOOOOOOOOOOO

Afterword by Dennis Cooper and Zac Farley

Dennis Cooper: When I was in poetry classes in college, there was this thing they used to call the Shakespeare Murders. There were all these young people who wanted to be poets, and then they'd be asked or forced to read Shakespeare and, once they did, they'd be like, "Forget it, I quit." Because Shakespeare's level of amazingness was too high. And then there were maybe one or two people who said, "Fuck Shakespeare."

Zac Farley: I'm gonna assume that was you?

Dennis Cooper: Basically. But when I was reading *Castle Faggot*, I had that kind of moment. I thought, "How did Derek do this? This is insane." I already knew Derek was a genius, but in this novel it's so pushed, it's so exploded or something. It was startling to see what happens to his voice when it's given so much more emotional drive. *Castle Faggot* has this fury in it and yet it's always meticulous and artistically over the top and extravagant.

Zac Farley: Faggotland seems like the best—and worst—but really the best place ever. The first part of the book, the flyer, makes it so palpable, I really want to go.

Dennis Cooper: But are you a faggot? I don't think you're really a faggot. Are you?

Zac Farley: But I would be if... Because that's the only way you get to go to the park. I would gladly impersonate one to get in.

Dennis Cooper: I guess I could fake it. But then there's a choice of being the sadist or the masochist 'cause, theoretically, one could also be an employee, no? One could be... Count, I forget his name.

Zac Farley: Count Choc-o-log. I don't know. He seems pretty solid. That part's taken.

Dennis Cooper: I would probably just go to the gift shop.

Zac Farley: Ultimately the materialist in me would just want the dollhouse which is just really nice of the book to offer.

Dennis Cooper: But I think you have to go all the way through the Castle to get to the gift shop, don't you?

Zac Farley: Or you can send cereal box tops. I think 50 box top coupons get you the dollhouse. Plus shipping.

Dennis Cooper: So the only other option is to eat breakfast cereal?

Zac Farley: A shit-ton of breakfast cereal.

Dennis Cooper: That would be very tough to do in France since the French aren't really into breakfast cereals. There are, like, five choices in the supermarkets and three of them are Corn Flakes. But I assume Derek knows that and that's all part of his novel's dastardly machinations. I mean, there's one store called the American Store by the Eiffel Tower, and they sell macaroni and cheese and Necco Wafers and they probably have Count Chocula and Lucky Charms and all of that. So I guess it would be possible but very expensive. So you would have to really, really want to go to Castle Faggot.

Zac Farley: You were saying something about the emotion and fury of Derek's voice in the book. I'm fascinated with the way the voice both changes radically from section to section and yet completely remains Derek McCormack's voice throughout, and how the location of his voice is so diversi-form. Even in the first section, the flyer, which weaponizes the kind of language found in a brochure to make it function like a VR headset if VR headsets actually worked and weren't just heavy things you put on your head, there are these injunctions: "Faggots!—kill yourselves!" At first that's where I placed his voice, but then there's the wizard, and a kid comes in which you can immediately tell is him, and a while later it actually is him. I think the injunctive voice is the one that most surprised me and excited me the most, too.

Dennis Cooper: But then he gets so evil.

Zac Farley: But he's just a kid.

Dennis Cooper: No, I mean Derek not the kid. Derek seems so innocent and sweet, but … You've probably never met him.

Zac Farley: No, I only know his work, I would love to meet him.

Dennis Cooper: I'm gonna tell you a story. One time when he visited LA, he and Jason McBride and I went to this mall that's right next to the Grauman's Chinese Theater. And suddenly, walking through the mall, was the actor who played Xander on *Buffy the Vampire Slayer*.

Zac Farley: I just re-watched some of *Buffy*. Xander's the worst.

Dennis Cooper: He was walking along with his girlfriend, and Derek saw him and went … I don't know how to describe it. His face got this demon possessed look, and he just suddenly jetted away at very high speed. Xander and his girlfriend were going up this escalator and Derek zoomed over and stood literally like…he put his chest right against their backs riding up the escalator. I saw Xander turn his head and bulge out his eyes like, "What the fuck?!" And we were like, "Oh my God." It was this really weird Derek we'd never seen before who was still innocent but also really scary. Then we just waited, and eventually Derek came down, and it didn't seem like Xander hit him because it was one of those situations where you felt like Xander was probably gonna hit him.

Zac Farley: He probably wanted that... to be hit.

Dennis Cooper: Maybe, maybe. I would say that's the only time that in my experiences with Derek where I thought, "Derek is kind of terrifying." So when I read this book, I thought, "This is that Derek coming out. That Derek has suddenly entered the world through his prose." So it wasn't as much of a shock to me as it will be to the usual Derek McCormack reader who will probably think, "What happened to Derek McCormack? I know he went through some hard stuff in his life, but this is not the Derek McCormack I'm used to at all." They'll probably be pretty freaked out.

Zac Farley: His prose is so amazing, it can do so many different things and it's so incredible at being whatever it is at any given point, and it's so... I mean, you can tell it's just been so fractured, and redone, and condensed that really, it's become haunted. There's all of this extraneous language, but it really needs to be there. The prose doesn't just describe the castle, it's also its architecture.

Dennis Cooper: It does everything it's doing in three-dimensions. Hard to describe.

Zac Farley: And that's what I mean with the architecture of the castle, and then the dollhouse, it's like they're the same space, and they're the same words used to describe them, but you really feel when he's describing Castle Faggot, it's really Castle Faggot. And when he's describing the dollhouse of

Castle Faggot, it's really the dollhouse, and they're radically different things, and they feel like different things.

Dennis Cooper: I pride myself on being able to understand how things work in fiction but Derek flummoxes me. He can use a staccato tone and beat in this way that's just amazing, and he de-homogenizes everything in his worlds and fancies it up at the same time, so his work has a unique crosshatched energy that I'm in awe of because…I don't know, his writing is so extremely particularised and ornate and ornamented, but, at the same time, his voice seems to come at you with such force, almost like it's being delivered through a public address system or something.

Zac Farley: I think that's what I mean with the injunctive voice. So intense, it's really beautiful.

Dennis Cooper: Yeah.

Zac Farley: And that's really strange, I mean really strange.

Dennis Cooper: At the same time, it's not writing that you think would work properly if it was read aloud. It's very much about the page and, in this case, about all those framed blanks, the squares and circles containing the non-illustrations, those are really important, even though I have no idea how they work. You think, "Okay, I get that this is a device," but then you keep looking at them and not wanting to see something in those spaces but thinking about what would be in those spaces and never imagining anything good enough. That's a remarkable thing too.

Zac Farley: We weren't sure for a second whether it was a placeholder or not, but it's so completely not a placeholder. It's so incredible that a blank space can ever be anything but a placeholder and it's not. It's not a cop out, it's really exactly like that. It's crazy, I don't even know how to talk about that or think about that. Only people without an imagination would try to imagine what they could look like.

For some of the books Derek McCormack has published, there has also been a hand made special edition, with objects. Do you think he's gonna make the dollhouse? I hope so.

Dennis Cooper: No doubt, and I don't think we're being paid to do this afterword thing so we should get it.

Zac Farley: We should get the castle dollhouse.

Dennis Cooper: I don't think Derek's ever been to France.

Zac Farley: The geography of Paris is really specific in the text, and seemingly correct. There's a section where Cocoa Chanel goes from Le Printemps to Galleries Lafayette and on to the Opera, stabbing, murdering, and swallowing all of the clothes on her way, and her path through the city from one place to the next makes total sense, it's all walking distance. I feel like it would be super dreamy to walk around in Paris with him.

Dennis Cooper: I've been trying to get Derek to come to Paris for years and years.

Zac Farley: I think we would learn a lot.

Dennis Cooper: He would love it here, he would never leave.

Zac Farley: But there are no haunted houses here, I don't know if he could handle that. We have to go to leave and go to Los Angeles every year for Halloween to see home haunts. Do you remember Camp Sherwood Scare, the haunted house about the nightmarish summer camp where all the kids are dead or missing, where your bunkmates stare at you all night with white masks, where the sleeping bags become body bags and archery isn't just an activity but a real threat?

Dennis Cooper: Yes, maybe the best home haunt ever. And we've been through hundreds, so we would know. It's also kind of a perfect point of comparison. Ignoring the difference that it was ultra-hetero and asexual and American, it similarly used a traditional, unassuming space, in its case a suburban garage and yard instead of "the novel," and employed every can of paint and computer print-out and old TV set and quickie make up job and piece of plywood that the family who made it could scrounge up to create this transcendent, disorienting experience. So, Castle Faggot-like except instead of dying at the hands of French fancy-pants, you waded through the blood and gore and wreckage of a slaughtered teen summer camp and escaped screaming. No gift shop though, sadly.

Zac Farley: In the front yard there was a tent, and in it a video projector that made it seem like two young girls were talking and singing face to face inside the tent, their shadows projected onto the side. I remember that illusion working really well and making me ecstatic, the surface projection on the side of the tent really did make the space inside of the tent come alive more than any actual kids could. And yet Castle Faggot is even better as a haunt than even Camp Sherwood Scare was.

Dennis Cooper: Not that you could actually graph out what Castle Faggot looks like at all by reading the book, even though the surfaces are extremely present.

Zac Farley: And the layers too, you know what is underneath and what it's smeared with, how it's been turned upside down and rotted. Its plasticity is really clear.

Dennis Cooper: Yeah, it's super clear. It's like a children's book or whatever. I mean, all of Derek's books are like children's books.

Zac Farley: Wow, it is a children's book, it really is. The best children's book ever.

Dennis Cooper: It's actually and weirdly the most like a children's book out of all his novels.

Zac Farley: And they all kind of try to be in a sense but this might be the most successful as a children's book.

Dennis Cooper: And at the same time it's rated X.

Zac Farley: I think you would need to get a really cool librarian to recommend it. Or some famous TV personality children look up to, if those still exist, or you know those kids on YouTube that do reviews of toys and stuff. There must be a kid on YouTube who reviews books, maybe. Or he should just get the ones who review the toys to review the book purely as an object. Which I feel would work. Just describing the book, how it functions as an object.

Dennis Cooper: It is really just one of the best books ever, and maybe the greatest novel ever written.

Zac Farley: But it also is, in a way, it's also the best dark ride, and the best theme park, the best TV special.

Dennis Cooper: It's more than a book. You're reading it, and you're like, "This isn't just a book. This is a magic spell, or this is an amusement park map."

Zac Farley: And it really is all of these things. It doesn't pretend to be or impersonate them, it actually is them. It's crazy. I love that constant shift where the characters are sometimes cartoons and sometimes animatronics—"fagimatronics!"—

and sometimes puppets or dolls. What he does with the surfaces becoming three-dimensional. That resonated with the text calling attention to itself as a material, like with the "fade to brown" and "wipe to" tricks. It's mind blowing.

Dennis Cooper: I think with the text, it does feel like you're reading with 3D glasses on. It does feel like the prose is actually in three dimensions, it's weird. 'Cause it's so sculptural, it's so incredibly sculptural and that's another thing, how did he do that? Is it just the right, somehow finessed mixture of color and language and the rhythm of the sentences and the exclamation points and … ?

Zac Farley: Yeah, maybe that's the thing, he's not a writer, he's a…

Dennis Cooper: What is he?

Zac Farley: He's an architect or something. I mean, that's demeaning but…

Dennis Cooper: Well, he could be a toy maker too, or he could be…

Zac Farley: Yeah, he's all of those.

Dennis Cooper: If you say he's an architect it feels too dry, or if you say he's a toy maker it sounds too dumb but…

Zac Farley: I don't know him, but it seems like it's a lot more personal than his other ones. I mean, sometimes you cringe reading it.

Dennis Cooper: I don't want to presume anything, but I agree that it feels very personal and it feels very…

Zac Farley: Emotional.

Dennis Cooper: Yeah, it's very angry. And that's interesting. 'Cause he's certainly been dark before, but this is really…

Zac Farley: It's probably dangerous, this book. But if it falls into the hands of children, as we're trying to devise, then it's safe, it will work.

Dennis Cooper: Children would really, really, really have to hide it really, really, really well from their parents. And they would have to put very heavy bedcovers over their head when they read it with a flashlight. Because parents would never understand this book. There are so few people of my age that I feel are worthy of this book.

Zac Farley: It's too good for adults.

Derek McCormack's previous books include *The Show That Smells* and *The Well-Dressed Wound* (Semiotext(e)).

Writer Dennis Cooper and visual artist/writer Zac Farley have collaborated on three feature films: *Like Cattle Towards Glow* (2015), *Permanent Green Light* (2018), and *Room Temperature* (forthcoming). In addition, Cooper is the author of ten novels, most recently *The Marbled Swarm* (Harper Perennial, 2012) and *I Wished* (Soho Press, 2021), as well as four books of fiction composed of animated GIFs, including the GIF novel *Zac's Drug Binge* (Kiddiepunk Press, 2020). Farley is currently collaborating on projects with French theater director/choreographer Gisele Vienne, most recently *Klara Kraus*, a mini-series for the French/ German television channel ARTE.